GOLDILOCKS
and the THREE
Potties

For the
BEST
little
Goldikids
in the
WOODS

Jodi
Sidney
Arthur
Bertie
Frieda
Herb

First published in 2017 by Nosy Crow Ltd, The Crow's Nest, 10a Lant Street, London SE1 1QR
www.nosycrow.com

ISBN 978 0 85763 923 3 (HB)
ISBN 978 0 85763 924 0 (PB)

Nosy Crow and associated logos are trademarks and/or registered trademarks of Nosy Crow Ltd.

Text and illustrations © Leigh Hodgkinson 2017
The right of Leigh Hodgkinson to be identified as the author and illustrator of this work has been asserted.

A CIP catalogue record for this book is available from the British Library.

Printed in China. Papers used by Nosy Crow are made from wood grown in sustainable forests.

10 9 8 7 6 5 4 3 2 1

GOLDILOCKS
and the THREE
Potties

Leigh
Hodgkinson

nosy crow

Once upon a time there was a **VERY** <u>little</u> girl called GOLDILOCKS who lived in a wood with her Mummy and Daddy.

Goldilocks was bored of wearing

soggy OLD

nappies

and thought that now would be

a good time to start wearing

BIG

girl

PANTS

for a change.

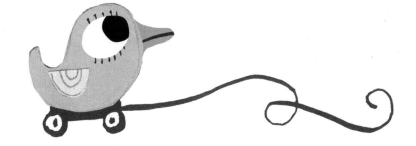

Big girl pants
that were not
too **frilly**...

Big girl pants
that were not
<u>too</u> SILLY...

Big girl pants that were

just right!

Now this Goldilocks
was a **clever** <u>little</u> **girl**.

She remembered that
if you wear pants and you need **a wee**...

you have to find *a potty* to wee **in.**

A potty that is not <u>too</u> BIG...

A potty that is not <u>too</u> small...

A potty that is

just right!

Sometimes Goldilocks thought she **really, really DID** need a wee . . .

Sometimes Goldilocks . . .   thought she **really** . . .

DIDN'T need a wee . . .   but then she did.

But soon enough,
Goldilocks . . .

got it . . .